Maria S. Porter

Recollections of Louisa May Alcott, John Greenleaf Whittier

and Robert Browning...

Maria S. Porter

Recollections of Louisa May Alcott, John Greenleaf Whittier and Robert Browning...

ISBN/EAN: 9783744708111

Printed in Europe, USA, Canada, Australia, Japan

Cover: Foto ©Andreas Hilbeck / pixelio.de

More available books at **www.hansebooks.com**

LOUISA MAY ALCOTT

At the Age of Twenty.

FROM AN UNPUBLISHED PORTRAIT IN POSSESSION OF MRS. PRATT.

ecollections of Louisa May Alcott, John Greenleaf Whittier, and Robert Browning, together with several memorial poems. Illustrated.

By

Maria S. Porter.

Published for the Author by
The New England Magazine Corporation.
1893.

CONTENTS.

RECOLLECTIONS OF LOUISA MAY ALCOTT.*

O name in American literature has more thrilled the hearts of the young people of this generation than that of Louisa May Alcott. What a life of beneficence and self-abnegation was hers! How distinctively was her character an outcome of the best New England ancestry! In her veins ran the blood of the Quincys, the Mays, the Alcotts, and the Sewalls. What better inheritance could one have? How important a factor in life is heredity! One is so enriched, strengthened, and upborne by a good ancestry, or sometimes, alas! so handicapped, baffled, and utterly defeated in the conflicts of life by bad hereditary influence, that when one has so fine an inheritance as was Louisa Alcott's, one should be thankful for it and rejoice in it as she did.

In looking back upon Miss Alcott's life, heroic and faithful to the end, it is the woman who interests us even more than the writer, whose phenomenal success in touching the hearts of old and young is known so well the world over. "Do the duty that lies nearest," was her life motto, and to its fulfilment were given hand and brain and heart. Helen Hunt Jackson once wrote of her, "Miss Alcott is really a benefactor of households." Truer words were never written. She was proud of her ancestors. I remember a characteristic expression of hers as we sat together one morning in June, 1876, in the Old South Meeting-House, where was assembled an immense audience stirred to a white heat of patriotic enthusiasm by the fervid eloquence of Wendell Phillips, whose plea to save that sacred landmark from the vandals who were ready to destroy it can never be forgotten. At the conclusion of Phillips's speech she turned to me, her face aglow

* Reprinted by permission of the New England Magazine Corporation.

with emotion, and said, "I am proud of my foremothers and fore-
fathers, and especially of my Sewall blood, even if the good old judge
did condemn the witches to be hanged." After a moment of silence
she added, "I am glad that he felt remorse, and had the manliness
to confess it. He was made of the right stuff." Of this ancestor,
Whittier wrote in "The Prophecy of Samuel Sewall": —

Amos Bronson Alcott.

"Stately and slow, with solemn air,
His black cap hiding his whitened hair,
Walks the Judge of the great Assize,
Samuel Sewall, the good and wise;
His face with lines of firmness wrought,
He wears the look of a man unbought."

Of the name of Quincy, Oliver Wendell
Holmes has written in "Dorothy Q": —

"Look not on her with eyes of scorn,
Dorothy Q was a lady born!
Ay! since the galloping Normans came,
England's annals have known her name;
And still to the three-hilled rebel town
Dear is that ancient name's renown,
For many a civic wreath they won,
The youthful sire and the gray-haired son."

Miss Alcott began to write at a very early age. Her childhood
and early girlhood were passed in the pure sweet atmosphere of a
home where love reigned. Louisa and her sister Anna were educated
in a desultory and fragmentary manner, or, perhaps one should say,
without system. Mr. and Mrs. Alcott, the two Misses Peabody,
Thoreau, Miss Mary Russell, and Mr. Lane had a share in their education. Mrs. Hawthorne taught Anna to read, and I think Louisa once
spoke of her to me as her own first teacher.

Mrs. Alcott was a remarkable woman, a great reader, with a broad
practical mind, deep love of humanity, wide charity, untiring energy,
and a highly sensitive organization, married to a man whom she de-
votedly loved, who was absolutely devoid of practical knowledge of
life, an idealist of the extremest type. With the narrowest means, her
trials, perplexities, and privations were very great, but she bore them
all with heroic courage and fidelity, and with unwavering affection for
her husband. Louisa early recognized all this. She soon developed the

6

distinguishing traits of both father and mother. Emerson, soon after he made Mr. Alcott's acquaintance, recognized his consummate ability as a conversationalist, and was through life his most loyal friend. Louisa was very proud of her father's intellectual acquirements, and it was most interesting to hear her tell of the high tributes paid him by some of the great thinkers of the age. In a note to me in October, 1882, just after her father had been stricken with paralysis, she wrote : —

Mrs. Alcott

"My poor dear father lies dumb and helpless. He seems to know us all; and it is so pathetic to see my handsome, hale, active old father changed at one fell blow into this helpless wreck. You know that he wrote those forty remarkable sonnets last winter, and these, with his cares as Dean of the School of Philosophy and his many lectures there, were enough to break down a man of eighty-three years. I continually protested and warned him against overwork and taxation of the brain, but 'twas of no avail. Wasn't I doing the same thing myself? I did not practise what I preached, and indeed I have great cause for fear that I may be some day stricken down as he is. He seems so tired of living; his active mind beats against the prison bars. Did I ever tell you what Mr. Emerson once said of him to me? 'Louisa, your father could have talked with Plato.' Was not that praise worth having? Since then I have often in writing addressed him as 'My dear old Plato.'"

Just after the publication of the " Correspondence of Carlyle and Emerson," I found her reading it one day. Her face was radiant with delight as she said: " Let me read you what Emerson wrote to Carlyle just before father went to England: ' I shall write again soon, for Bronson Alcott will probably go to England in about a month, and him I shall surely send you, hoping to atone by his great nature for many smaller ones that have craved to see you.'" Again she read: "' He is a great man and is made for what is greatest.' . . . . ' Alcott has returned to Concord with his wife and children and taken a cottage and an acre of ground, to get his living by the help of God and his own spade. I see that some of the education people in England have a school called " Alcott House," after my friend. At home here he is despised and rejected of men as much as ever was Pestalozzi. But the creature thinks and talks, and I am proud of my neighbor.'"

7

ORCHARD HOUSE, CONCORD.
The Home of the "Little Women."

Carlyle's estimate of Alcott, although not as high as Emerson's, was a fairly appreciative one. He wrote to Emerson after Alcott's visits to him : —

" He is a genial, innocent, simple-hearted man, of much natural intelligence and good-ness, with an air of rusticity, veracity, and dignity withal, which in many ways appeals to me. The good Alcott, with his long, lean face and figure, his gray, worn temples and mild radiant eyes, all bent on saving the world by a return to the Golden Age; he comes before one like a kind Don Quixote, whom nobody can even laugh at without loving."

Louisa, after reading these extracts, taken from different parts of the books, said with emphasis : " It takes great men like Emerson and Carlyle and Thoreau to appreciate father at his best." She always spoke with great freedom and frankness of her father's lack of prac-tical ability; and very pathetic were some of the stories she told of her own early struggles to earn money for the family needs; of her

8

strivings to smother pride while staying with a maternal relative who had offered her a home for the winter while she was teaching in a small private school in Boston; and of her indignation when Mr. Fields said to her father, who had taken a story of hers to him to read with the hope that it might be accepted for the *Atlantic*: "Tell Louisa to stick to her teaching; she can never succeed as a writer!" This message, she said, made her exclaim to her father: "Tell him I will succeed as a writer, and some day I shall write for the *Atlantic!*" Not long afterward a story of hers was accepted by the *Atlantic* and a check for fifty dollars sent her. In telling me of this she said: "I called it my happy money, for with it I bought a second-hand carpet for our parlor, a bonnet for Anna, some blue ribbons for May, some shoes and stockings for myself, and put what was left into the Micawber Railroad, the Harold Skimpole Three Per Cents and the Alcott Sinking Fund."

One merry talk about the experiences of her girlhood and early womanhood, with several pathetic stories that she told me one moonlight summer evening, as we floated down the Concord River, made a profound impression, and I recall them with great distinctness.

"When I was a girl of eighteen or thereabouts," she said. "I had very fine dark brown hair, thick and long, almost touching the floor as I stood. At a time when the family needs were great, and discouragement weighed heavily upon us, I went to a barber, let down my hair, and asked him how much money he would give me for it. When he told me the sum, it seemed so large to me that I then and there determined I would part with my most precious possession if during the next week the clouds did not lift."

This costly gift, however, was not laid upon the family altar by the heroic girl. A friend, who was ever ready to extend an unobtrusive helping hand when it was needed, came to the rescue. Louisa, in relating this, said, "That was not the first time he had helped father, nor was it indeed the last."

Another incident that she told me that same evening in her inimitable way, with all its amusing and pathetic details, revealed to me how supreme was her loyalty and devotion to her family, and above all to her mother.

THE PORCH OF THE ORCHARD HOUSE.

From a Drawing by May Alcott Nieriker.

In 1850, when Louisa was eighteen years of age, Mrs. Alcott had, with the advice of friends, taken a position as visitor to the poor in Boston. She had also opened an intelligence office, where she often assisted gentlefolk, reduced from affluence to poverty, to situations where, without an entire sacrifice of pride, they could earn an honest independence. One day as Louisa was sitting in the office sewing on some flannel garments for the poor, under her mother's supervision, a tall man, evidently from his garb a clergyman, entered and said that he came to procure a companion for his invalid sister and aged father. He described the situation as a most desirable one, adding that the companion would be asked to read to them and perform the light duties of the household that had formerly devolved upon his sister, who was a martyr to neuralgia. The companion would be in every respect treated as one of the family, and all the comforts of home would be hers.

Mrs. Alcott, who, in spite of many bitter experiences in the past, never lost her faith in people and was rather too apt to take them for what they seemed to be, tried to think of some one who would be glad of so pleasant a home as described. She turned to Louisa and asked her if she could suggest any one. The reply came at once, "Only myself!" Great was her mother's surprise, and she exclaimed, "Do you really mean it, dear?" "I really do, if Mr. R—— thinks I would suit." The clergyman smiled and said, "I am sure you would, and I feel that if we can secure you, we shall be most fortunate."

When Mrs. Alcott had recovered from her surprise, she prudently asked him what wages would be paid. The smooth reply was that the word "wages" must not be used, but any one who lent youth and strength to a feeble household would be paid and well paid, and with another smile he took his leave. Then Mrs. Alcott asked, "Are you in earnest in engaging to go out for a month to live with these utter strangers?"

"Of course I am," said Louisa. "Why not try the experiment? It can but fail, as the teaching and sewing and acting and writing have. I do housework at home for love; why not there for money?"

"But you know, dear," her mother replied, "it is going out to service, even if you are called a companion."

" I don't care. Every kind of work that is paid for is service. It is rather a downfall to give up trying to be a Siddons or a Fanny Kemble, and become a servant at the beck and call of people; but what of it?" " All my highly respectable relatives," said Louisa, " held up their hands in holy horror when I left the paternal roof to go to my place of servitude, as they called it, and said, 'Louisa Alcott will disgrace her name by what she is doing.' But despite the lamentations and laughter of my sisters, I got my small wardrobe ready, and after embracing the family, with firmness started for my new home."

She had promised to stay four weeks; but, after a few days, she found that instead of being a companion to the invalid sister, who was a nonentity, while the father passed his days in a placid doze, she was called upon to perform the most menial services, made a mere household drudge, or, to use her own expression, " a galley slave." " Then," said she, " I pocketed my pride, looked the situation squarely in the face, and determined I would stay on to the bitter end. My word must be as good as my bond." By degrees all the hard work of the family was imposed upon her, for the sister was too feeble to help or even to direct in any way, and the servant was too old to do anything but the cooking, so that even the roughest work was hers. Having made up her mind to go when the month was over, she brought water from the well, dug paths in the snow, split kindlings, made fires, sifted ashes, and was in fact a veritable Cinderella. " But," said she, " I did sometimes rebel, and being a mortal worm, I turned now and then when the clergyman trod upon me, especially in the matter of bootblacking, — that was too much for my good blood to bear! All the Mays, Sewalls, and Alcotts of the past and present appeared before my mind's eye; at blacking boots I drew the line and flatly refused. That evening I enjoyed the sinful spectacle of the reverend bootblack at the task. Oh, what a long month that was! And when I announced my intention of leaving at its end, such dismay fell upon the invalid sister, that I consented to remain until my mother could find a substitute. Three weeks longer I waited. Two other victims came, but soon left, and on departing called me a fool to stay another hour. I quite agreed with them, and when the third substitute came, clutched my possessions, and said I should go at once. The sister wept, the father tremblingly expressed regret, and the clergyman washed his hands of the whole affair by shutting himself in his study. At the last moment, Eliza, the sister, nervously tucked a small pocket-book into my hand, and bade me good by with a sob. The old servant gave me a curious look as I went away, and exclaimed, 'Don't blame us for anything: some folks is liberal and some ain't!' So I left

THE WAYSIDE.

From a Drawing by May Alcott Nieriker.

the house, bearing in my pocket what I hoped was, if not a liberal, at least an honest return for seven weeks of the hardest work I ever did. Unable to resist the desire to see what my earnings were, I opened my purse — and beheld four dollars! I have had many bitter moments in my life, but one of the bitterest was then, when I stood in the road that cold, windy day, with my little pocket-book open, and

13

BUST OF MISS ALCOTT.

Made by Walton Ricketson for the Concord Library

looked from my poor, chapped, grimy, chilblained hands to the paltry sum that had been considered enough to pay for the labor they had done. I went home, showed my honorable wounds, and told my tale to the sympathetic family. The four dollars were returned, and one of my dear ones would have shaken the minister, in spite of his cloth, had he crossed his path."

This experience of going out to service at eighteen made so painful an impression upon her that she rarely referred to it, and when she did so it was with heightened color and tearful eyes.

Long years before she wrote her story called "Transcendental Wild Oats," she had told me in her humorous way of the family experiences at "Fruitlands," as the community established by Mr. Alcott and his English friend, Mr. Lane, was called. In 1843, when Louisa was eleven years of age, these idealists went to the small town of Harvard, near Lancaster, Massachusetts, to carry out their theories. Mr. Lane was to be the patriarch of the colony of latter-day saints. Louisa, in speaking of her father's connection with this movement, said: "Father had a devout faith in the ideal. He wanted to live the highest, purest life, to plant a paradise where no serpent could enter. Mother was unconverted, but true as steel to him, following wherever his vagaries led, hoping that at last she might, after many wanderings, find a home for herself and children."

The diet at Fruitlands was strictly vegetarian; no milk, butter, cheese, or meat could be eaten or tasted even within the holy precincts — nothing that had caused death or wrong to man or beast. The garments must be of linen, because those made from wool were the result of the use of cruel shears to rob the sheep of their wool, and the covering of the silkworms must be despoiled to make silken ones. The bill of fare was bread, porridge, and water for breakfast; bread, vegetables, and water for dinner; bread, fruit, and water for supper. They had to go to bed with the birds, because candles, for conscientious reasons, could not be burnt, — the " inner light " must be all-sufficient: sometimes pine knots were used when absolutely necessary. Meanwhile, the philosophers sitting in the moonlight built with words a new heaven and a new earth, or in the starlight wooed the Oversoul, and lived amid metaphysical mists and philanthropic pyrotechnics. Mr. Alcott revelled in the "Newness," as he was fond of calling their new life. He fully believed that in time not only Fruitlands, but the whole earth would become a happy valley, the Golden Age would come; and toward this end he talked, he prophesied, he worked with his hands; for *he* was in dead earnest, his was the enthusiasm of a soul too high for the rough usage of this workaday world.

In the mean while, with Spartan fortitude Mrs. Alcott bore the brunt of the household drudgery. How Louisa's eyes would twinkle as she described the strange methods at Fruitlands! "One day in autumn mother thought a northeast storm was brewing. The grain was ripe and must be gathered before the rain came to ruin it. Some call of the Oversoul had wafted all the men away, and so mother, Anna, a son of Mr. Lane's, and I must gather the grain in some way. Mother had it done with a clothes-basket and a stout Russia linen sheet. Putting the grain into the basket we emptied it upon the sheet, and taking hold of the four corners carried it to the barn."

May Alcott Nieriker.

During the summer Mr. Emerson visited them and wrote thus in his journal: —

"The sun and the sky do not look calmer than Alcott and his family at Fruitlands. They seem to have arrived at the fact — to have got rid of the show, and so are serene. Their manners and behavior in the house and in the field are those of superior men, — of men of rest. What had they to conceal? What had they to exhibit? And it seemed so high an attainment that I thought — as often before, so now more, because they had a fit home or the picture was fitly framed — that those men ought to be maintained in their place by the country for its culture. Young men and young maidens, old men and women, should visit them and be inspired. I think there is as much merit in beautiful manners as in hard work. I will not prejudge them successful. They look well in July; we will see them in December."

But alas! Emerson did not see the idealists in December. When the cold weather came on, the tragedy for the Alcott family began.

Some of those who had basked in the summer sunshine of the "New-ness" fled to "fresh fields and pastures new" when the cold and dark days came. Mr. Lane, in whose companionship Mr. Alcott had en-joyed so much, left to join the Shakers, where he soon found the order of things reversed for him, as it was all work and no play with the brethren and sisters there. Mr. Alcott's strength and spirits were exhausted. He had assumed more than his share of responsibility,

MISS ALCOTT'S HOUSE AT NONQUITT.

and a heavy weight of suffering and debt was laid upon him. The experiment had ended in disastrous failure, — his Utopia had vanished into thin air. His strange theories had alienated many of his old friends; he was called a visionary, a fool, a madman, and some even called him unprincipled. What could he do for his family? Then it was that his wife, whose loyalty was supreme, whose good sense and

17

practical views of life had shown her from the beginning what would be the outcome of the experiment, then it was that her strong right arm rescued him. He was cherished with renewed love and tenderness by wife and children, who always remembered with pain this most bitter of all their experiences, and could never refer to it without weeping. Louisa, in recalling it, would say: "Mother fought down despondency and drove it from the household, and even wrested happiness from the hard hand of fate."

THE CONCORD RIVER.

After Mr. Alcott had rallied from the depression caused by the failure at Fruitlands, he went back to Concord with his family and worked manfully with his hands for their support; he also resumed his delightful conversations, which in those days of transcendentalism had become somewhat famous. When a young girl, I attended them with my mother at the house of the Unitarian clergyman in Lynn. The talks of Mr. Alcott and the conversations that followed were most interesting — unlike anything that had been heard in Lynn or its vicinity in those days. Afterward, Ralph Waldo Emerson and Thoreau used to come and give us in parlors "Lectures on Transcendentalism," as they were called.

The busy years rolled on for Louisa, who exerted herself to the utmost to be the family helper in sewing, teaching, and writing. After her stories were accepted by the *Atlantic*, it became for her smooth sailing. One day, as Mr. Alcott was calling upon Longfellow, the poet took up the last *Atlantic* and said, "I want to read to you Emerson's fine poem on Thoreau's Flute." As he began to read, Mr. Alcott interrupted him, exclaiming with delight, "My daughter Louisa wrote that!" In telling me of this, Louisa said, "Do you wonder that I felt as proud as a peacock when father came home and told me?" This occurred before the names of the writers were appended to their contributions to the magazine.

Bust of Alcott in Boston _____ the Concord Library

Miss Alcott made two visits to Europe, travelling quite extensively and meeting many distinguished people. She was always an ardent admirer of the writings of Dickens, and she had the great pleasure of meeting him in London and hearing him read. All the characters in his books were like household friends to her; she never tired of talking about and quoting him. Her impersonation of Mrs. Jarley was inimitable; and when I had charge of the representation of "The Old Curiosity Shop" at the Authors' Carnival held at Music Hall, in aid of the Old South Preservation

Fund, I was so fortunate as to persuade her to take the part of Mrs. Jarley in the waxwork show. It was a famous show, never to be forgotten. People came from all parts of New England to see Louisa Alcott's Mrs. Jarley, for she had for years been famous in the part whenever a deserving charity was to be helped in that way. Shouts of delight and peals of laughter greeted her original and witty descriptions of the "figgers" at each performance, and it was repeated every evening for a week.

No. 10 Louisburg Square, Boston.

One day during her last illness I received a note from her, in which she wrote : —

"A poor gentlewoman in London has written to me, because she thinks after reading my books that I loved Dickens's writings, and must have a kind heart and generous nature, and, therefore, takes the liberty to write and ask me to buy a letter written to her by Charles Dickens, who was a friend of hers. Such is her desperate need of money that she must part with it, although it is very precious to her. She has fourteen children, and asks five pounds for the letter. Now, I don't want the letter, and am not well enough to see or even write to any one about buying it from her; will not you try and do it for me? 'If at first you don't succeed, try, try again.' I'll add something to whatever you get for it. Remember the poor thing has fourteen children, and has been reduced from affluence to poverty."

The letter could not be sold for the price named, nor indeed to any one at its proper value, so Miss Alcott returned it and sent the price asked for it by the next steamer. This is only one of the many generous acts of sympathy of which I knew.

The Alcotts were always anti-slavery people. Mrs. Alcott's brother, Samuel J. May, and her cousin, Samuel E. Sewall, were the stanchest supporters of Garrison in the early struggles. Mr. Alcott was the firm friend of that intrepid leader in the war against slavery. Nearly all the leading Abolitionists were their friends, — Lucretia Mott, the Grimké sisters, Theodore Weld, Lydia Maria Child, Wendell Phillips, Theodore Parker, Miss Peabody, and others of that remarkable galaxy of men and women who in those benighted years were ranked as fanatics by the community at large. When the mob spirit reigned in Boston and Garrison was taken to a jail in the city to protect him from its fury and save his life, Mr. and Mrs. Alcott were among the first to call upon him to express their sympathy.

When the war came, the Alcotts were stirred to a white heat of patriotism. Louisa wrote : —

"I am scraping lint for our boys in blue. My May blood is up. I must go to the front to nurse the poor helpless soldiers who are wounded and bleeding. I MUST GO, and good by if I never return."

She did go, and came very near losing her life; for while in the hospital she contracted a typhoid fever, was very ill, and never recovered from its effects; it can be truly said of her she gave her life to her country. One of her father's most beautiful sonnets was written in reference to this experience. He refers to her in this as " Duty's faithful child."

During her experience as a hospital nurse she wrote letters home and to the *Commonwealth* newspaper. From these letters a selection was made and published under the title of " Hospital Sketches." To me this is the most interesting and pathetic of all Miss Alcott's

21

books. With shattered health she returned to her writing and her home duties. Slowly but surely she won recognition; but it was not until she had written "Little Women," that full pecuniary success came.

Miss Alcott had the keenest insight into character. She was rarely mistaken in her judgment of people. She was intolerant of all shams, and despised pretentious persons. Often in her pleasant rooms at the Bellevue have I listened to her estimates of people whom we knew. She was sometimes almost ruthless in her denunciation of society, so called. I remember what she said as we sat together at a private ball, where many of the butterflies of fashion and leaders of society were assembled. As with her clear, keen eyes she viewed the pageant, she exclaimed: "Society in New York and in Boston, as we have seen it to-night, is corrupt. Such immodest dressing, such flirtations of some of these married women with young men whose mothers they might be, so far as age is concerned, such drinking of champagne — I loathe it all! If I can only live long enough I mean to write a book whose characters will be drawn from life. Mrs. —— [naming a person present] shall be prominent as the society leader, and the fidelity of the picture shall leave no one in doubt as to the original."

She always bitterly denounced all unwomanliness. Her standard of morality was a high one, and the same for men as for women. She was an earnest advocate of woman suffrage and college education for girls, because she devoutly believed that woman should do whatever she could do well, in church or school or state. When I was elected a member of the school committee of Melrose in 1874, she wrote: —

"I rejoice greatly thereat, and hope that the first thing that you and Mrs. Sewall propose in your first meeting will be to reduce the salary of the head master of the High School, and increase the salary of the first woman assistant, whose work is quite as good as his, and even harder; to make the pay equal. I believe in the same pay for the same good work. Don't you? In future let woman do whatever she can do; let men place no more impediments in the way; above all things let's have fair play, — let *simple justice* be done, say I. Let us hear no more of 'woman's sphere' either from our wise (?) legislators beneath the State House dome, or from our clergymen in their pulpits. I am tired, year after year, of hearing such twaddle about sturdy oaks and clinging vines and man's chivalric protection of woman. Let woman find out her own limitations, and if, as is so confidently asserted, nature has defined her sphere, she will be guided accordingly; but in heaven's name give her a chance! Let the professions be open to her; let fifty years of college education be hers, and then we shall see

22

what we shall see. Then, and not until then, shall we be able to say what woman can and what she cannot do, and coming generations will know and be able to define more clearly what is a 'woman's sphere' than these benighted men who now try to do it."

During Miss Alcott's last illness she wrote :—

"When I get upon my feet I am going (D. V.) to devote myself to settling poor souls who need a helping hand in hard times."

Many pictures and some busts have been made of Miss Alcott, but very few of them are satisfactory. The portrait painted in Rome by Healy is, I think, a very good one. The bas-relief by Walton Ricketson, her dear sculptor friend, is most interesting, and has many admirers. Ricketson has also made a bust of Mr. Alcott for the Concord Library, which is exceedingly good, much liked by the family, and so far as I know, by all who have seen it. Of the photographs of

House on Dunreath Place, Boston, where Miss Alcott died.

Miss Alcott only two or three are in the least satisfactory, notably the full-length one made by Warren many years ago, and also one by Allen and Rowell. In speaking of her pictures she once said, "When I don't look like the tragic muse, I look like a smoky relic of the Boston fire." Mr. Ricketson is now at work upon a bust of her, a photograph of which, from the clay, accompanies this article. In a letter to me in reply to one written after I had seen the bust in his studio at Concord, Mr. Ricketson writes :—

"I feel deeply the important task I have to do in making this portrait, since it is to give form and expression to the broad love of humanity, the fixed purpose to fulfil her mission, the

23

womanly dignity, physical beauty, and queenly presence which were so perfectly combined in our late friend, and all so dominated by a fine intellectuality. To do this and satisfy a public that has formed somewhat an idea of her personal appearance is indeed a task worthy of the best effort. I certainly have some advantages to start with. The medallion from life modelled at Nonquitt in 1886, and at that time considered the best likeness of her, is invaluable, as the measurements are all accurate. I also have access to all the photographs, etc., of the family, and the criticisms of her sister, nephews, and friends, and my long and intimate acquaintance. I feel this to be the most important work I have as yet attempted. I intend to give unlimited time to it, and shall not consider it completed until the family and friends are fully satisfied. The success of the bust of the father leads me to hope for the same result in the one of his beloved daughter."

Miss Alcott always took a warm interest in Mr. Frank Elwell, the sculptor, and assisted him towards his education in art.

Miss Alcott had a keen sense of humor, and her friends recall with delight her sallies of wit and caustic descriptions of the School of Philosophy, the "unfathomable wisdom," the "metaphysical pyrotechnics," the strange vagaries of some of the devotees. She would sometimes enclose such nonsense rhymes as these to her intimate friends : —

> "Philosophers sit in their sylvan hall
> And talk of the duties of man,
> Of Chaos and Cosmos, Hegel and Kant,
> With the Oversoul well in the van;
> All on their hobbies they amble away,
> And a terrible dust they make;
> Disciples devout both gaze and adore,
> As daily they listen, and bake!"

The "sylvan hall" was, as I know from bitter experience while attending the sessions of the School of Philosophy, the hottest place in historic old Concord.

Sometimes Miss Alcott would bring her nonsense rhymes or "jingles," as she called them, to the club, and read at our pleasant club-teas, amid shouts of merriment followed by heartiest applause, such clever bits as the following : —

A WAIL UTTERED IN THE WOMAN'S CLUB.

God bless you, merry ladies,
May nothing you dismay,
As you sit here at ease and hark
Unto my dismal lay.

Get out your pocket-handkerchiefs,
Give o'er your jokes and songs,
Forget awhile your Woman's Rights,
And pity author's wrongs.

There is a town of high repute,
  Where saints and sages dwell,
Who in these latter days are forced
  To bid sweet peace farewell;
For all their men are demigods, —
  So rumor doth declare, —
And all the women are De Staëls,
  And genius fills the air.

So eager pilgrims penetrate
  To their most private nooks,
Storm their back doors in search of news
  And interview their cooks,
Worship at every victim's shrine,
  See halos round their hats,
Embalm the chickweed from their yards,
  And photograph their cats.

There's Emerson, the poet wise,
  That much-enduring man,
Sees Jenkinses from every clime,
  But dodges when he can.
Chaos and Cosmos down below
  Their waves of trouble roll,
While safely in his attic locked,
  He woos the Oversoul.

And Hawthorne, shy as any maid,
  From these invaders fled
Out of the window like a wraith,
  Or to his tower sped —
Till vanishing from this rude world,
  He left behind no clue,
Except along the hillside path
  The violet's tender blue.

Channing scarce dares at eventide
  To leave his lonely lair;
Reporters lurk on every side
  And hunt him like a bear.
Quaint Thoreau sought the wilderness,
  But callers by the score
Scared the poor hermit from his cell,
  The woodchuck from his door.

There's Alcott, the philosopher,
  Who labored long and well
Plato's Republic to restore,
  Now keeps a free hotel;
Whole boarding-schools of gushing girls
  That hapless mansion throng,
And Young Men's Christian U-ni-ons,
  Full five-and-seventy strong.

Alas! what can the poor souls do?
  Their homes are homes no more;
No washing-day is sacred now;
  Spring cleaning's never o'er.
Their doorsteps are the stranger's camp,
  Their trees bear many a name,
Artists their very nightcaps sketch;
  And this — and this is fame!

Deluded world! your Mecca is
  A sand-bank glorified;
The river that you see and sing
  Has "skeeters," but no tide.
The gods raise "garden-sarse" and milk
  And in these classic shades
Dwell nineteen chronic invalids
  And forty-two old maids.

Some April shall the world behold
  Embattled authors stand,
With steel pens of the sharpest tip
  In every inky hand.
Their bridge shall be a bridge of sighs,
  Their motto, " Privacy ";
Their bullets like that Luther flung
  When bidding Satan flee.

Their monuments of ruined books,
  Of precious wasted days,
Of tempers tried, distracted brains,
  That might have won fresh bays.
And round this sad memorial,
  Oh, chant for requiem :
Here lie our murdered geniuses;
  Concord has conquered them.

From the time that the success of " Little Women " established her
reputation as a writer, until the last day of her life, her absolute devotion to her family continued. Her mother's declining years were

25

soothed with every care and comfort that filial love could bestow; she died in Louisa's arms, and for her she performed all the last offices of affection, — no stranger hands touched the beloved form. The most beautiful of her poems was written at this time, in memory of her mother, and was called, " Transfiguration." A short time after her mother's death, her sister May, who had married Mr. Ernest Nieriker, a Swiss gentleman, living in Paris, died after the birth of her child. Of this Louisa wrote me in reply to a letter of sympathy : —

"I mourn and mourn by day and night for May. Of all the griefs in my life, and I have had many, this is the bitterest. I try so hard to be brave, but the tears will come, and I go off and cry and cry; the dear little baby may comfort Ernest, but what can comfort us? May called her two years of marriage perfect happiness, and said : 'If I die when baby is born, don't mourn, for I have had in these two years more happiness than comes to many in a lifetime.' The baby is named for me, and is to be given to me as my very own. What a sad but precious legacy ! "

The little golden-haired Lulu was brought to her by its aunt, Miss Sophie Nieriker, and she was indeed a great comfort to Miss Alcott for the remainder of her life.

In 1886, Miss Alcott took a furnished house on Louisburg Square in Boston, and although her health was still very delicate she anticipated much quiet happiness in the family life. In the autumn and winter she suffered much from indigestion, sleeplessness, and general debility. Early in December she told me how very much she was suffering, and added, "I mean if possible to keep up until after Christmas, and then I am sure I shall break down." When I went to carry her a Christmas gift, she showed me the Christmas tree, and seemed so bright and happy that I was not prepared to hear soon after that she had gone out to the restful quiet of a home in Dunreath Place, at the Highlands, where she could be tenderly cared for under the direction of her friend, Dr. Rhoda Lawrence, to whom she dedicated one of her books. She was too weak to bear even the pleasurable excitement of her own home, and called Dr. Lawrence's house, "Saint's Rest." The following summer she went with Dr. Lawrence to Princeton, but on her return in the autumn her illness took an alarming character, and she was unable to see her friends, and only occasionally the members of her family. On her last birthday, November 29, she received many gifts, and as I had remembered her, the follow-

A PORTION OF MISS ALCOTT'S LAST LETTER.

ing characteristic letter came to me, the last but one that she sent me : —

"Thanks for the flowers and for the kind thought that sent them to the poor old exile. I had seven boxes of flowers, two baskets, and three plants, forty gifts in all, and at night I lay in a room that looked like a small fair, with its five tables covered with pretty things, borders of posies, and your noble roses towering in state over all the rest. That red one was so delicious that I revelled in it like a big bee, and felt it might almost do for a body — I am so thin now. Everybody was very kind, and my solitary day was made happy by so much love. Illness and exile have their bright side, I find, and I hope to come out in the spring a gay old butterfly. My rest-and-milk-cure is doing well, and I am an obedient oyster since I have learned that patience and time are my best helps."

THE ALCOTT LOT IN SLEEPY HOLLOW CEMETERY, CONCORD.

In February, 1888, Mr. Alcott was taken with what proved to be his last illness. Louisa knew that the end was near, and as often as she was able came into town to see him. On Thursday morning, March 2, I chanced to be at the house, where I had gone to inquire for Mr. Alcott and Louisa. While talking with Mrs. Pratt, her sister, the door opened, and Louisa, who had come in from the Highlands to see her father, entered. I had not seen her for months, and the sight of her thin, wan face and sad look shocked me, and I felt for the first

27

time that she was hopelessly ill. After a few affectionate words of greeting she passed through the open doors of the next room. The scene that followed was most pathetic. There lay the dear old father, stricken with death, his face illumined with the radiance that comes but once, — with uplifted gaze he heeded her not. Kneeling by his bedside, she took his hand, kissed it and placed in it the pansies she had brought, saying, "It is Weedy" (her pet name). Then after a moment's silence she asked, "What are you thinking of, dear?" He replied, looking upward, "Up there; you come too!" Then with a kiss she said, "I wish I could go," bowing her head as if in prayer. After a little came the "Good by," the last kiss, and like a shadow she glided from the room. The following day I wrote her at the "Saint's Rest," enclosing a photograph of her sister May, that I found among some old letters of her own. Referring to my meeting with her the day before, I said: —

"I hope you will be able to bear the impending event with the same brave philosophy that was yours when your dear mother died."

She received my note on Saturday morning, together with one from her sister. Early in the morning she replied to her sister's note, telling of a dull pain and a weight like iron on her head. Later, she wrote me the last words she ever penned; and in the evening came the fatal stroke of apoplexy, followed by unconsciousness. Her letter to me was a follows: —

"DEAR MRS. PORTER, — Thanks for the picture. I am very glad to have it. No philosophy is needed for the impending event. I shall be very glad when the dear old man falls asleep after his long and innocent life. Sorrow has no place at such times, and death is never terrible when it comes as now in the likeness of a friend.

"Yours truly,

"L. M. A.

"P. S. I have another year to stay in my 'Saint's Rest,' and then I am promised twenty years of health. I don't want so many, and I have no idea I shall see them. But as I don't live for myself, I hold on for others, and shall find time to die some day, I hope."

Mr. Alcott died on Sunday morning, March 4, and on Tuesday morning, March 6, death, "in the likeness of a friend," came to Louisa. Mr. Alcott's funeral took place on Tuesday morning, and many of the friends there assembled were met with the tidings of Louisa's death. Miss Alcott had made every arrangement for her funeral. It was her desire that only those near and dear to her should be present, that the service should be simple, and that only friends should take part. The services were indeed simple, but most impressive. Dr. Bartol, the lifelong friend of the family, paid a loving and simple tribute to her character, as did Mrs. Livermore. Mrs. Cheney read the sonnet written by Mr. Alcott, which refers to her as " Duty's faithful child." Mrs. Harriet Winslow Sewall, a very dear cousin, read with her sweet voice and in a tender manner that most beautiful of Louisa's poems, "Transfiguration," written in memory of her mother. I had carried my simple tribute of verse, but could not control voice or emotion sufficiently to read it, and laid it with a bunch of white Cherokee roses on the casket.

JOHN GREENLEAF WHITTIER

JOHN GREENLEAF WHITTIER.

THAT John Greenleaf Whittier was the most beloved of our poets, the tributes paid him over the length and breadth of our land show. Born on a rugged New England farm, he was reared in Quaker simplicity and integrity of life, from which he never deviated. In speech and dress he adhered to the Quaker form. There have been greater and more scholarly American poets, of wider fame, but as a poet of nature, of New England life and legends, was he not the sweetest singer of all? The very atmosphere of New England permeates his verse. In loyalty to right and freedom, no one has equalled him. He has often been called the Burns of New England, and last summer Lord Tennyson, in speaking of Whittier's poem, "My Playmate," said, "It is a perfect poem," adding, "in some of his descriptions of scenery and wild flowers, he would rank with Wordsworth"; and he repeated, in his sonorous voice, that exquisite verse from "The Daffodils," ending with —

> "And then my heart with pleasure fills
> And dances with the daffodils."

What vivid word-pictures Whittier gives us, not only of New England scenery, but of the prairies of the West, the luxuriance of the South, the tropics, of Rome, and of Venice

> "When the pomp of sunrise waits
> On Venice at her watery gates."

His sun has set, but what a glow of beauty lingers around the hills and lakes and streams of Massachusetts and New Hampshire, that he loved so well and dwelt amid so long! His songs among the hills flow with the melody of brooks, the sweep of torrents, the roar of cascades, are impressive with the grandeur of mountains, the splendor of autumnal trees, the glory of sunsets, and vibrate with poetic strength and beauty. His thrilling lyrics and stirring anti-slavery poems won for him early in life the name of the "Poet of Freedom." Edwin P. Whipple, our most famous literary critic and essayist, was one of the first to recognize Whittier as a poet of great power. Mr. Whittier once said to him, "I have always been grateful to thee, Edwin, for from thee I first won recognition; and although I was partly conscious of what in me lay, thy assurance gave me courage to go on with my work." To Edwin and Charlotte Whipple he dedicated a volume of his poems. How much his songs, "In War Time," dedicated to Samuel E. and Harriet Winslow Sewall, did to strengthen the patriotism of the North during the darkest hours of the national struggle, all of us who lived and suffered through the horrors of those years love to recall. How precious were his tender memorial verses to our young heroes like Shaw, Winthrop, Lowell,

Whittier's Birthplace, Haverhill, Mass.

Putnam, and others who gave their lives to their country! His tribute to the brave Gen. Bartlett ranks among the best of these. Was ever poem more scathing in its denunciation of a wrongdoer than "Ichabod," written in 1850, just after Daniel Webster had made his famous "seventh of March speech," in the Senate of the United States, in favor of the infamous Fugitive Slave Law? In what high regard Ralph Waldo Emerson held this poem, an incident that took place at the celebration of the seventieth birthday of Whittier will show. The publishers of the *Atlantic Monthly* gave a dinner in honor of the occasion; among those present were many of Whittier's friends among the poets, Longfellow, Holmes, Emerson, and others. Many brought their congratulations in verse. When Emerson was called upon by the chairman he said, as nearly as I can recollect: "I have brought no poem of my own for my friend's birthday, but I will read one of his that reflects more honor upon him than anything I could have written in his praise"; and he read, as only he could read, the poem of "Ichabod." Those who were present will long remember the scene, which should not be lost to history. This poem expresses the intense severity with which Whittier and the Abolitionists regarded the action of Daniel Webster. His friends at the North, and especially the "Webster Whigs" (so called) of Boston, indorsed his speech. After the wicked bill became a law, they were willing, alas! and ready to enforce it, and return to their cruel masters the poor, trembling colored men and women who, through perils and suffering inexpressible of mind and body, had escaped from bondage. They were willing, also, to make of Massachusetts a hunting ground for slaves; to make of her what Whittier had, in his spirited "Massachusetts to Virginia," declared *she never should become!*

> "For us and for our children the vow which we have given
> For freedom and humanity is registered in heaven;
> No slave hunt in our borders, no pirate on our strand!
> No fetters in the Bay State, no slave upon our land!"

These lines should stand side by side with Lowell's immortal ones: —

> "Truth forever on the scaffold, wrong forever on the throne,
> Yet that scaffold sways the future, and behind the dim unknown
> Standeth God within the shadow, keeping watch above his own."

Who that saw that day of shame in Boston can ever forget it, when the Court House was encircled with chains by order of the United States marshal, and the judges of the Supreme Court of Massachusetts were obliged to stoop under this symbol of the supremacy of the slave-holders in order to reach their tribunals of justice? The day of the deepest humiliation for Boston was that when Thomas Sims was marched down State Street, a file of soldiers on either side, to the vessel that was to convey him back to stripes and servitude. What lessons of man's inhumanity to man did those benighted days afford! Not once only, but twice, in utter disregard of the higher law that should hold sway over men and nations, were fugitive slaves dragged back from Boston to the homes of their oppressors.

The excitement of the Abolitionists was very great at the time; many concealed the fugitives in their houses or barns at the greatest risk. A relative of mine concealed a slave named Latimer in the attic of his house for weeks; and Mrs. Alcott, so her daughter Louisa used to relate, had two fugitives hidden in her house, a woman and man. The woman was in the attic, and the man, whenever the slave-catchers were supposed to be in pursuit, was put into a large, old-fashioned brick oven and shut in until the danger was past. Those indeed were troublous times! Whittier wrote his most intense and remarkable verses of appeal and warning during those years. His was a righteous indignation at his country's wrongdoing, and shame at the recreant Northern statesmen, who in servile fear bent their necks to wear the yoke of the slave power. When other poets, with the shining exception of Lowell, were silent or nearly so, he had won a place in the hearts of the friends of humanity, whose love for him grew stronger and deeper as the years rolled on.

Whittier's friendship for Garrison began from the time that his first poem was published in a newspaper that Garrison edited in Newbury-port. On January 1, 1831, the first number of the *Liberator* was published in Boston by William Lloyd Garrison, whose name the world will never forget as one of the greatest of philanthropists. This leader of the anti-slavery movement, from the strength of his moral conviction that slavery was a gigantic sin, determined early in life to do all that he could to destroy it — to demand its abolition. In his salutatory address to the public in the *Liberator* he wrote, in words that have often been quoted and should never be forgotten: "I am aware that many object to the severity of my language, but is there not cause for severity? I WILL BE as harsh as truth, and as uncompromising as justice! On this subject I do not wish to think, or speak, or write with moderation. No! no! urge me not to use moderation in a cause like the present. I am in earnest; I will not equivocate; I will not retreat a single inch, — AND I WILL BE HEARD!" In reply to a letter from the South asking questions about Garrison's incendiary utterances in the *Liberator*, Harrison Gray Otis, the mayor of Boston, wrote of the office of the *Liberator*, "It is an obscure hole"; but James Russell Lowell, of blessed memory, wrote thus of it: —

> "In a small chamber, friendless and unseen,
>   Toiled o'er his types one poor, unlearned young man;
>   The place was dull, unfurnitured, and mean,
>   But there the freedom of a race began."

Whittier at the same time wrote his well-known poem, "To W. L. G.," and was from the first a sympathizer and helper; and so was Samuel E. Sewall, a young lawyer of Boston, in whose office the anti-slavery society was formed. Ellis Gray Loring, Gamaliel Bradford, and others were present at the second meeting in December, and joined. A little later Wendell Phillips and Edmund Quincy became members, and were ever after zealous in the good work. At the time of the Garrison mob in Boston, Whittier, who was at that time a representative in the General Court, came down from the State House and witnessed the disgraceful scene of the mob, which was described in one of the newspapers and referred to as "composed of gentlemen in broadcloth, of property and standing." After Garrison had been carried to jail to protect his life from the fury of the mob, Whittier, Mr. Sewall, Mr. and Mrs. Bronson Alcott, and other sympathizing friends visited him, and talked with him through the bars of his cell. On the way home, Mrs. Alcott took from the house of a friend the portrait of George Thompson (divested of its frame), concealed it beneath her cloak, and kept it hidden in her house until it was safe to show it. In 1837, Elijah P. Lovejoy was murdered at Alton, Ill., while defending his printing press from a mob assembled to destroy it, his offence being that of printing editorials

35

against slavery. In the week following a meeting was called in Faneuil Hall to protest against the violation of the principle of liberty in the murder of Lovejoy. Dr. William Ellery Channing made a most impressive speech in favor of free speech and of liberty for the press, and George S. Hillard spoke next. He was to have been followed by Wendell Phillips, but the floor was taken by James T. Austin, the attorney general of Massachusetts, who in speaking of the murdered Lovejoy said that he "died as the fool dieth," and that the men who killed him were as great patriots as those who threw the tea into Boston Harbor. He was applauded by a part of the audience, and when Wendell Phillips ascended to the platform he was hissed and hooted by the crowd. In spite of the outcries and opposition of the audience, he held his place as firm as the granite rock, and sternly rebuked Austin for his speech. "When I heard the gentleman," said he, "lay down the principles that placed the murderers at Alton side by side with Otis and Hancock, with Quincy and Adams, I thought those pictured lips," pointing to their portraits, "would have broken into voice to rebuke the recreant American, the slanderer of the dead."

Whittier always referred to, that "maiden speech" of Phillips as most impressive in its eloquence, and said the scene should be painted to go down to posterity as of historic importance. From that hour Wendell Phillips ranked as the greatest of our orators.

My personal recollections of Whittier date back to my early girlhood. I saw him first at an anti-slavery fair in Boston, where my aunt was, with others, in charge of a table. I had as a child a great desire to see Whittier and all the rest of those intrepid leaders in the good cause. The people of whom I had read and heard so much were all there, — Garrison and his noble wife, Whittier, the Sewalls, Edmund Quincy, Wendell Phillips, the Mays, the Bowditches, the Westons, James Russell Lowell and his beautiful *fiancée*, Maria White, Lydia Maria Child, Mrs. Chapman, and many more of those who were working in dead earnest to abolish the "sum of all villanies," — slavery. I recognized Whittier as soon as he entered the hall from his Quaker dress and the shyness of his manner. He was tall, very erect, with glowing dark eyes, dark brown hair, a fine complexion. As he approached our table, he espied some

36

volumes of the "Liberty Bell," and took one up to examine its contents, asked the price, and said he would take two copies; when I gave him the books I said, "I thank thee," whereupon he asked, "Art thou a Quaker?" I told him that I often used the "plain language" when talking with my Quaker relatives. In answer to his questioning, I told him my grandmother was a birthright member and at one time clerk of the women's meeting; thereupon we had a chat about my Quaker relatives in Salem, and I found that he knew them well.

"THE SWIFT POWOW."

All through the years that followed, I saw him occasionally up to the time of his last birthday, the 17th of December. On that day he looked so pale and wan, so thin, and evidently was so enfeebled, I had a premonition I should never see him again, should never more look upon his face or grasp his hand.

For many years I was in the habit of meeting Whittier when he was the guest of our mutual friends, the Sewalls, at their delightful home in Melrose. He was very fond of "the dear Sewalls," as we were wont to call them. "A sweeter woman ne'er drew breath" than

37

Harriet Winslow Sewall, and some of her poems Mr. Whittier very often quoted, especially the "Wild Columbine," and the one beginning,

"Why thus longing — thus forever sighing?"

which is in nearly all the collections of American poetry.

Sometimes when Whittier was a guest in their pleasant home in Melrose, they would invite some of their old friends and his to meet him. I remember one goodly company that sat around the fire one evening long ago, and told stories and experiences of the days that tried men's souls. Whittier, Garrison, Wendell Phillips, Lydia Maria Child, Lucretia Mott, Theodore Weld, were there. Garrison, who had had the most bitter experience of all, his life often imperilled, a price set upon his head by the exasperated Southerners, told us of some indignities that he had suffered, that were untold before, even to those who, like Whittier and Sewall, had helped him with pen and purse from the first. Some of us were startled at the revelations he made that memorable evening. Phillips, too, told his stories of infuriated mobs and social ostracism. "Boston gave me the cold shoulder," said he, "from the hour when in Faneuil Hall I rebuked James T. Austin; and Boston also ostracized Charles Sumner for his position against slavery, to her everlasting shame be it spoken!" Mrs. Child told us of the discourteous action of the trustees of the Boston Athenaeum in withdrawing from her the complimentary ticket to make use of the library and gallery, bestowed upon her after she had written "Philothea." The occasion of this act of most reprehensible rudeness was owing to her having written a book against slavery!

Whittier related an account of a mob that he encountered in New Hampshire, with a friend of his whose name I forget. They barely managed to escape, and years afterward he met a stranger who introduced himself and confessed to him with deepest contrition that he was the ringleader of that mob, and that if he had not escaped with his friend they would have been tarred and feathered! He also told us some ludicrous incidents and stories of the "come-outers," as they were called, and of those "inevitable lunatics" that always appeared, like Abby Folsom (that "flea of conventions" as Emerson called her) and Father Lamson, with his huge Sairey Gamp umbrella, who

38

brandished it as they harangued the crowd at the conventions. I
recall one story at which we all laughed heartily, and Whittier most
of all as he told it. "We had a meeting in Tremont Temple, a very
stormy one; the speakers had been scathing in their denunciations of
slaveholders, and recreant Northern statesmen in Congress. There
were many bitter pro-slavery men in the audience; the mob spirit was
aroused; it looked as if blood might be shed. Garrison, whose
head was as bald then as it is now, sat on the platform beside William
H. Burleigh, whose hair fell in heavy masses to his shoulders. A negro
sat near them, who wished to speak, but the noisy mob would not allow
it. Suddenly, during a lull in the uproar, a man in the back of the hall
shouted, 'Mr. Speaker, Mr. Speaker, I have only a word to say. I
want that negro to shave Burleigh, and make a wig for Garrison!'
Immediately the whole audience burst into roars of laughter and shouts
of applause, which had the effect to avert the danger that seemed immi-
nent to the speakers, and they were allowed to go on with the meeting."
One other story he told, saying that he had written so much he had
forgotten a great deal of it, and as an illustration said: "I once went
to hear a famous orator, and he ended his speech with a poetical quota-
tion. I clapped my hands with all my might, and the person next me
touched me on the shoulder and asked if I knew who wrote that
verse. 'No, I don't,' I replied; 'but it's good!' It seems I had written
it myself." After this story the whole company vied with each other
in telling amusing incidents of bygone years. Of that famous company only one is living, Theodore D. Weld. Mr. Whittier was among
the first advocates of woman suffrage, and was ever one of the honored
officers of the Woman Suffrage Association, of which James Freeman
Clarke, George William Curtis, Thomas Wentworth Higginson, William
Ingersoll Bowditch, Lucy Stone, Julia Ward Howe, have been presi-
dents. Whittier was a lifelong friend of Lucy Stone, holding her in the
highest esteem, not only for what she had done for woman suffrage,
but for her earlier work in behalf of the slave, when she went from
city to city and from town to town to lecture against slavery, encoun-
tering obloquy, the fury of mobs, brutal insults from brutal men, un-
flinchingly walking in the thorny path of duty. On the occasion of the
celebration of her sixtieth birthday I wrote an enthusiastic tribute in

39

verse, in which I referred to the first time I saw her, and to an incident of the evening when she laid her hand in blessing on the dusky brow of an escaped slave woman, whose story she had told so eloquently as to make the profoundest impression. This incident took place in Faneuil Hall in 1849. Mr. Whittier, having read the verses in a newspaper, wrote thus: "I write to thank thee for thy tribute to Lucy Stone. I have always had a great admiration for her. She is worthy of all that thee say of her in thy fine poem."

From the formation of the Republican party he was its staunch supporter, and always made an especial effort to vote. It was a great grief to him that some of his dearest friends, with lifelong devotion to humanity and the right, should leave the Republican party, whose record, both before and after the war, had been that of which they all had a right to be proud. To leave that party because corruption had crept in and corrupt men had been placed in office, and affiliate with a party whose Southern leaders and Northern "copperheads" had plunged the nation into all the horrors of a civil war, whose record on the slavery question had been so bad a one, seemed to him inexplicable. "Why did they not stay in our party and reform it, instead of joining one so much more corrupt?" he exclaimed to me one day in the summer of 1884. That the sons of Garrison, that Samuel Sewall, that Freeman Clarke, Lowell, Higginson, had "gone over to the enemy," as he expressed it, gave him great pain.

The return of Mr. Sewall to the Republican fold gladdened his heart, and when the *Transcript* swung back to the Republican side he rejoiced greatly. Who can forget the letters of Whittier and Edward Everett Hale addressed to the Republicans during the campaign of 1884? After the election of Cleveland in November, I received the following letter from Whittier: —

"DANVERS, 11th mo. 22d, 1884.

"DEAR FRIEND, — I ought to have thanked thee before for thy graceful and kind verses, — a tribute, I fear, quite undeserved.

"I quite agree with thee in deploring the folly of the Independents. I could not read Sewall's letter or James Freeman Clarke's speeches! and the suicidal course of the Prohibitionists vexes me. But for them Blaine would have been elected. What a combination of rum-sellers and the John-Johns! I am greatly sorry for the defeat of Cabot Lodge; but Massachusetts, on the whole, has done well, for which let us be thankful.

"I am truly thy friend,

"JOHN G. WHITTIER."

Soon after the death of Whittier I heard a sermon from a well-known clergyman of the Unitarian faith, in which he called attention to the fact that nearly if not all of our great poets were Unitarians, viz., Bryant, Longfellow, Emerson, Lowell, Holmes. Whittier, if we may use the expression, was a Unitarian or Hicksite Quaker, as was Lucretia Mott, who was so broad and so opposed to the doctrine of the so-called Orthodox Friends that in some quarters she was ostracized and regarded as a heretic.

In a recent letter, Oliver Wendell Holmes has written the most beautiful and tender tribute to Whittier. He says of his influence on the religious thought of the American people: " It has been far greater, I believe, than that of the occupant of any pulpit. It is not by any attack upon the faith of any Christian fellow-ship that he did service for the liberal thought of our community. . . . Of late years I have been in close sympathy with him, not es-pecially as an Abolitionist, not merely through human sympathies, but as belonging with me to the 'Church with-out a Bishop,' which seems

Whittier's Last Resting Place.

the natural complement of a 'State without a King.' I mean the church which lives by no formula, which believes in a loving Father and trusts him for the final well-being of the whole spiritual universe which he has called into being. John Greenleaf Whittier reached the hearts of his fellow-countrymen, especially of New-Englanders para-lyzed by the teachings of Edwards, as Burns kindled the souls of Scotchmen palsied by the dogmas of Thomas Boston and his fellow-sectaries. When Whittier preaches his lifelong sermon in 'Songs of

Oct. 19th 1892

Dear Mr Porter

I thank you for
your kind and interesting
note. I am glad that my
letter about Whittier meets
your approval. In the midst
of the doctrinal fights and squabbles
going on all around us it is
good to remember the sweet lessons
of charity for all kinds of beliefs and
honest unbeliefs which filled the
loving soul of John Greenleaf Whittier.

Very truly Yours

O W Holmes.

Love and Hope,' I think of the immortal legacy he has left his countrymen, and repeat his own words as applied to Roger Williams: —

> ' Still echo in the hearts of men
> The words that thou hast spoken;
> No forge of hell can weld again
> The fetters thou hast broken.
>
> ' The pilgrim needs a pass no more
> From Roman or Genevan;
> Thought-free no ghostly tollman keeps
> Henceforth the road to heaven.' "

In reply to my note written to Dr. Holmes after reading this tribute to Whittier, he wrote: "I am glad that my letter about Whittier met your approval. In the midst of the doctrinal fights and squabbles going on all around us, it is good to remember the sweet lessons of charity for all kinds of beliefs and honest unbeliefs which filled the loving soul of John Greenleaf Whittier."

Soon after Whittier had written "The Eternal Goodness," I wrote him that it contained my creed. In reply he wrote: " I am glad that ' The Eternal Goodness ' contains thy creed. Others have written me the same. I am not much of a sectarian and care little for creeds, but I do love to hear the Quaker speech and see the Quaker dress. ' My heart warms to the Tartan.' "

My presentiment on his last birthday proved a true one. I never saw Whittier again. When I returned from Europe I heard of his illness and then of his death, which took place on September 7, 1892. He died peacefully in serene faith, surrounded by loving relatives, and on a perfect autumn day his worn-out frame was laid beside the dust of his mother and sister. In his own tender words from " Snow-Bound " we can say : —

> " How many a poor one's blessing went
> With thee beneath the low green tent."

ROBERT BROWNING.

ROBERT BROWNING IN HIS HOME.

URING the summer of 1889 I was the guest of an acquaintance in London who had been the lifelong friend of Robert Browning and his sister; and when she asked me who were the people I cared most to meet in England, I replied instantly, "Robert Browning and Mr. Gladstone."

The sister-in-law of my hostess (the Countess of Rothes) was the Miss Haworth to whom so many of the letters of Browning were written and first given to the public in Mrs. Sutherland Orr's "Life of Robert Browning." Miss Haworth's exquisite pen-and-ink illustrations of some of Mrs. Browning's poems were hung upon the walls of her sister's drawing-room, and were among her priceless art treasures. Miss Haworth died many years before Browning, and he spoke with tender regret of her loss. As I look back upon the summer of 1889 in London, two red-letter days appear in my calendar of enjoyment: one is that of the golden wedding of Mr. and Mrs. Gladstone; the other, that on which I first saw Robert Browning in his charming home, for it was indeed a great pleasure to see him there, so kindly was the cordial greeting, so genuine the hospitality. Miss Browning, his sister, who ever after the death of his wife presided over his household, bore a great resemblance to him, and was a most interesting person. It was through her kind invitation that I visited there. The home of the Brownings was in South Kensington, No. 29 De Vere Gardens. The house was a large one, and most artistically and attractively furnished. The library, with the collection of rare books and art treasures of the poet, was of the greatest interest. The drawing-room was spacious, and hanging upon the walls were soft-hued tapestries. Much of the furniture was of Venetian make and beautifully carved. There were many fine old pictures, and some by distinguished modern painters. Of several busts, that of Mrs. Browning, by William W. Story, was most noticeable; a bowl of rare china was always beside it, filled with flowers. The tables were covered with books, and calling my attention to them, Mr. Browning said: "I have many friends among the authors, and they kindly send me copies of their books; it keeps me very busy to read them all; however, I do all that I can in that direction. I wish they were all as good as this one of Wentworth Higginson's. Do you know him?" I replied that I had known him many years, and liked him and his writings exceedingly. Then he said, "When you go home, tell him I said he was not only a charming poet, but a charming fellow to know." He asked many questions about the people whom he knew in Boston, and spoke with warm interest of some of them, especially of Dr. Holmes, expressing profound sympathy for him in the crushing grief which had befallen him in the loss of his wife and daughter since his visit to England. "How desolate he must be!" he exclaimed; "Mrs. Sargent was so devoted to her father, and was such a cheery little woman!" He talked much of Longfellow, Emerson, and of Hawthorne and his wife. "What a remarkable person Mrs. Hawthorne was, and Una was *almost* a genius. After Mrs. Hawthorne's death I went very often to see Una and Rose, to assist them in arranging their father's manuscript for publication." After relating some interesting incidents about the family, he added, "All those Hawthorne children had marked ability. How could it be otherwise, with such a parentage?"

He spoke most affectionately of James Russell Lowell, and of his delight in his writings. "The Commemoration Ode" he regarded as one of his best poems, "The Present Crisis" was another, and he repeated the line,

"Truth forever on the scaffold, wrong forever on the throne,"

with great expression, adding, "That has the heroic ring: that line will live!" He warmly praised the "Biglow Papers" for their humor, and asked, "Are you familiar with the poem he wrote at the time of his first wife's death, called 'After the Burial'?" I replied that I knew every word of it. "Will you be kind enough to repeat it, I cannot recall it all?"   After I had done so, he was silent for a moment, and then with much feeling exclaimed, " That's a great poem ; what a wail of despair, but how deep and true it is ! "   " Did you ever see Maria Lowell?" he asked.   I told him I used to see her occasionally in the days of the anti-slavery warfare, that I had never forgotten her face, and added, " Its great beauty was that of expression." " So I have been told," he replied ; " and speaking of beauty, I must show you a photograph of my son's wife."   He then showed me photographs of his son and daughter-in-law.   When I expressed my admiration of the latter, he gave them both to me, and said : " If you show them to any of my friends in Boston, say that one does not get the faintest idea from the photograph of the beauty of her coloring or of the lovely tints of her hair.   She is an American, and we are very proud of her.   She is a descendant of Gov. Paddington, and has good blood in her veins."

I was, of course, delighted to have the photographs, but like Oliver Twist, I dared to ask for " more " !   I ventured to inquire if he had a good picture of himself, and if I might see it.   Miss Browning replied, " Yes, we have one just taken ; it is the best one he has had for years, and if you like it you shall have one."   After looking at it I said, " It is the best I have ever seen, the eyes and the expression are wonderfully good."   As Mr. Browning was writing his name and the date under it, he said, " If you show this to Dr. Holmes, tell him the old fellow looks like that now."   The next week when I was there at five-o'clock tea he gave me another photograph, a much larger one, in profile ; and although that is interesting, the smaller one is better as a likeness.   In looking over my autograph album he made running comments on the poets as he read, Parsons, Whittier, Holmes, Aldrich, Mrs. Howe, Helen Hunt, Mrs. Deland, Howells, Boyle O'Reilly, and all the rest of them.   " What verse of mine shall I write?"   When I replied, I should like something from " Rabbi Ben Ezra," he wrote : —

> " All that is at all
> Lasts ever past recall :
> Earth changes, but thy soul and God stand sure."

He wrote this on the page opposite to that on which Longfellow had written a translation from the Italian:—

"Che sembra mi alma, doves amor non stanza.
Casa di notte senza foco, o face."

Longfellow's translation runs:—

"The soul, where love abideth not, resembles
A house by night without or fire or torch."

The soul, where love abideth not, resembles
A house by night, without or fire or torch.

Che sembra mi' alma, doves amor non stanza,
Casa di notte, senza foco, o face.

Henry W. Longfellow

FACSIMILE OF LONGFELLOW'S COUPLET.

When he caught sight of Longfellow's lines, he exclaimed, "Longfellow didn't make the rhyme. I'll try my hand at it." And as quick as thought wrote:—

"What seems a soul where Love's outside the porch,
A house by night with neither fire nor torch."

Saying gleefully, "I've done it: there's my rhyme!"

He asked me one day if I belonged to a Browning Club, and was greatly amused when I told him I belonged to two, one that met weekly, — a club of ladies, to read and study his poems,— and another that met monthly at the Brunswick, having a membership of nearly two hundred, and of which his friend Col. T. W. Higginson was the affable and accomplished president. In reply to his questionings, I told him of some of the fine essays and readings we had listened to there, notably those from Mr. Hayes and Mr. Riddle. It was then he said,

All that - is it all

Lasts ever (that exists :
Earth changes, but thy soul and God stand sure.

"

from Rabbi Ben Ezra.

Robert Browning .

July 30. '89 . (_____)

" From all that I have heard from my friends in Boston, they regarded Mr. Levi Thaxter as the best reader and interpreter of my poems you have had there. Did you know him?" My reply was that I had attended his readings for years. He was much amused with the picture sent him from Boston representing an Englishman who was approaching Boston in a railway train, asking the conductor, " What is this strange sound I hear?" the conductor's reply was, " Oh ! that is the Bostonians reading Browning."

He was very proud of the work of his son, who is devoted to art, and showed me a portrait of himself, which I did not like, and another of his friend Alfred Dommett, of whom he wrote as " Waring." This he seemed especially to like, and told me how precious it was to him. As he looked at the " counterfeit presentment " of the friend who was so dear to him, and told me of the " irreparable loss," his eyes filled with tears and his voice was tremulous with emotion. One day when I went in after a walk he said, " You have just missed Miss———" (a mutual acquaintance), " she has been here more than an hour." I replied impulsively, " I'm glad she has gone, she is such a bore !" " Yes," he said, " she is a bore, but my sister and I bear with her because she loved that dear woman so," — pointing to Story's bust of his wife.

Browning's portrait has been painted by many artists, but of all that I saw in England, I liked best the one by Watts, and that painted by Felix Moschelles is next in merit. If Sir John Millais could have painted as fine a portrait of Browning as is his of Gladstone (which was painted for some of the ladies of England, to present to Mrs. Gladstone on their golden wedding day), what a treasure it would be for this generation and those that are to come ! In speaking of his father, Browning said : " I inherit my vigor of constitution from him. He had a remarkable physique, and he lived to the age of eighty-four, without ever having had a day's illness. My father helped me to do my best. When I think of so many authors who have had to struggle with such gigantic difficulties, I have very little reason to be proud of my achievements. My path was smoothed for me by my father's assistance. He always had the courage of his convictions, and he sacrificed a fortune to them ; he so hated slavery that he left India on that ac-

In speaking of the Browning Clubs in this country, he said, "It gives me great pleasure to hear how many people are reading and studying my poems"; then with a twinkle in his eye he said, "One good woman over there, she was not from Boston, however, covered four sheets with questions,— did I mean this, or this, or that (always wide of the mark, I assure you),— and at last ended with a charge of obscurity, and asked if I would write and tell her what I did mean in certain poems which she named. I never intend to be discourteous to any earnest inquirer, but I did not reply to *her* letter." He delighted to recall the stories he had heard from some of his friends who had struggled so hard to understand his "Sordello," and would relate the funniest ones with great glee. He told me that Mrs. Carlyle confessed to him that she had tackled the book and had been ignominiously baffled in her attempt to comprehend it, and also said Carlyle wrote to him, "My wife has read through 'Sordello' without being able to make out whether Sordello was a man, or a city, or a book!" He had been told that Tennyson had tried to read it, and in bitterness of spirit admitted that there were only two lines in it that he understood, and they were both lies; they were the opening and the closing ones.

> "Who will, may hear Sordello's story told,"

and

> "Who would, has heard Sordello's story told."

When I told him that those stories were quite new to me, but that I had heard the very amusing one told of Douglas Jerrold and his wife, he laughed heartily and exclaimed, "That is the best story of all." In regard to the charge so often made against him of wilful obscurity, he once wrote: "Having hitherto done my utmost in the art to which my life is a devotion, I cannot engage to increase the effort, but I conceive there may be helpful light as well as reassuring warmth in the attention and sympathy I gratefully acknowledge."

It is now forty-five years since I first heard a poem of Browning's read. It was ".A Blot in the Scutcheon." So full of power and pathos was it that I was profoundly impressed. I have since heard it read often and often, but the masterly interpretation of it by Levi Thaxter stands out most vividly in my memory. I can recall every tone of his voice, every shade of feeling as he spoke, with a sob in his throat, those thrilling words of Mildred's:—

> "I — I was so young!
> Besides I loved him — Thorold, and I had
> No mother; God forgot me: so I fell."

In 1842, Charles Dickens, to whom John Forster had sent the manuscript of ".A Blot in the Scutcheon" to read, wrote: "Browning's play has thrown me into a perfect passion of sorrow. To say that there is in its subject anything save what is lovely, true, deeply affecting, full of the best emotion, is to say there is no light in the sun and no heat in blood. I know nothing that is so affecting, nothing in any book I have ever read, as Mildred's recurrence to that, 'I was so young! . . . I had no mother.' Tell Browning that I believe from my soul there is no man living (and not many dead) that could produce such a work." This was written by Dickens to Forster forty-nine years ago, long before Browning's genius had found recognition. To-day all the great thinkers of the age have crowned him with laurel. Arch deacon Farrer told me last summer that he ranked him as the great Christian poet of the century. This is surely high praise from one of the greatest preachers of England. Cannot Browning be called with truth the poet of humanity? He has indeed measured the heights and sounded the depths. In dramatic delineation of the subtle phases of human experience, of the passions, joys, and woes of life, who can equal him? One of the finest tributes ever paid him was that of his old friend, Walter Savage Landor, to whom his devotion was so great : —

> "Since Chaucer was alive and hale,
> No man has walked our roads with step
> So active, so inquiring eye, or tongue
> So varied in discourse."

Browning's faith in immortality, and in the Power which is his ex pression for Divine Love, is best given in that remarkable poem entitled " Reverie," where these lines occur : —

> " I have faith such end shall be;
> From the first Power was — I knew.
> Life has made clear to me
> That, strive for but clearer view
> Love were as plain to see."

What vigor there is in that marvellous Epilogue, the last poem that he wrote : —

> " One who never turned his back, but marched breast forward,
>   Never doubted clouds would break,
>   Never dreamed, though right were worsted, wrong would triumph,
>   Held we fall to rise, are baffled to fight better,
>   Sleep to wake.

> " No, at noonday in the bustle of man's work time
>   Greet the unseen with a cheer!
>   Bid him forward, breast and back as either should be —
>   ' Strive and thrive ' cry Speed — fight on — fare ever
>   There as here!"

The most beautiful of all his poems was written shortly after his wife's death, and called " Prospice." His unshaken belief in reunion after death is given full expression in the last lines : —

"Then a light, then thy breast
O thou soul of my soul, I shall clasp thee again,
And with God be the rest."

For versatiliy, Browning has been by many of his admirers ranked next to Shakespeare. His learning was so wide, so profound, in a word he was so great, that he will hold a very high place in the final judgment of literature, in English poetry. Although some of his work is open to the charge of obscurity, yet all through his poems are verses which are as limpid as any of Shelley's or those of Keats. Some of his lyrics are clear, vivid word-pictures that are not at all above the ordinary understanding. How many children have listened spellbound to the "Pied Piper of Hamelin," or with delight to "How they brought the Good News from Ghent to Aix"; beautiful "Evelyn Hope," the songs of Pippa, "Oh! to be in England now that April's there," are poems as clear as sunlight and familiar as household words in countless homes the wide world over.

Browning's powers were unimpaired to the last hour of his life. In the autumn of 1889 he went to Venice, fair Venice, that he loved so well, and there on December 12, 1889, he died in the arms of his beloved son, in the light of a world-wide fame. His flower-laden bier, followed by a fleet of gondolas, floated in the pomp of sunlight through the "watery gates of Venice" to the Chapel of Saint Michael, where the casket was placed temporarily. Later his grave was made in Westminster Abbey, just below Chaucer's, and near to Spencer's resting place. England's greatest and best were assembled in the dim, vast aisles of the sacred Abbey to do honor to the great poet. One of the most impressive features of the service was the chanting by that world-famous choir of Mrs. Browning's beautiful poem, "He giveth His Beloved Sleep." Outside the Abbey a vast crowd was assembled; there were his humble admirers, the artisans, the poor workers of London, who came with their flowers and sprigs of laurel to throw before the hearse. One pathetic incident showed the affectionate regard in which he was held by the workingmen. A wan-faced, hollow-eyed man was seen to shiver with emotion and timidly pull from his sleeve a large white chrysanthemum, throwing it before the coffin as it was borne inward, then weeping passionately he disappeared into the crowd.

Memorial Poems.

LOUISA MAY ALCOTT.

Rememb'ring all her past,
Heroic to the last,
" Weep not for her," we said,
" The noble woman dead."

Nor mourn we, but rejoice,
And with unfaltering voice,
The vapor we call life
Vanished, — and all the strife

With pain, relentless thorn,
That of the flesh is born,
The heritage of earth,
Besetting us from birth.

Ere Death's sharp summons blew,
Each warning pang she knew,
Willing to die, or live,
Her life to others give.

She won the true success,
She lived to love, to bless;
Faithful unto the end,
Farewell, beloved friend.

Humanity's great woes
Exchanged for heaven's repose;
A spirit's glad release,
To never-ending peace.

With one she held so dear,
Translated to that sphere
Whose glory none may tell;
With her — with him — 'tis well.

March 8, 1888.

JOHN GREENLEAF WHITTIER.

No purer record have we seen
    Than his upon whose bier to-day
With mourning hearts and reverent mien
    These lilies white and fair we lay;

Fit types are they of spotless life
    Through nearly fourscore years and ten,
With every manly virtue rife,
    Peaceful, yet strong with speech and pen.

His verse is known in every land;
    By countless lips his hymns are sung;
From Bay State to Pacific strand
    His words have like a prophet's rung.

When Slavery's cloud, so fraught with fate,
    Hung black upon the nation's sky,
From Casco Bay to Golden Gate
    Was heard a spirit-stirring cry;

And notes of warning, clear and strong,
    Rang out when Whittier grasped the pen,
Till Right, triumphant over Wrong,
    Upraised the slaves and made them men.

Through seas of blood and Treason's hate,
    Justice at last o'ercame her foe;
Still did his pen their wrongs relate,
    That rights of freemen they should know.

No smallest leaf can we to-day
    Add to the green of laurel crown,
Only our grateful tribute pay
    To one who meekly wore renown,

And tell how much his songs have wrought
    In hours of pain and days of gloom,
What balm, what blessing they have brought,
    How filled our lives with light and bloom.

Can sculptor carve or limner paint
    "The Hero" as his pen hath done,
The "Cadmus of the blind," the saint
    Who light from deepest darkness won;

The lovely "Playmate" 'neath the pine —
    "The pines so dark on Ramoth hill" —
The bashful boy who fed the kine
    And plucked the flowers of Folly Mill?

We see the sweetbrier and the flowers,
    And hear the moaning of the pines,
And singing through the golden hours
    The birds atilt on swaying vines.

We see the dear New England home,
    The tender scenes in "Snow-Bound" given;
The tyrant 'neath Saint Peter's dome,
    Whose papal cloak his scorn hath riven

Till all men view his hidden wrong
    Who bound on Rome her "cast-off weight" —
A figure drawn in colors strong,
    Forever for the world to hate.

"Eternal Goodness" holds a creed
    Embodied in a holy hymn
To comfort hearts in sorest need
    When eyes with grief and loss are dim.

How vain the effort to rehearse
    His gifts to us of tongue and pen —
The wondrous power of his verse,
    His lifelong work for fellow-men.

In loyalty to all that's good,
    In stern rebuke of every wrong,
And manly faith in womanhood,
    Without a peer he stands in song.

ROBERT BROWNING.

By land and sea 'twas flashed to every shore,
  From fair old Venice the sad tidings spread,
England's great poet is, alas ! no more,
  World-wide the grief for Robert Browning dead !

Dead ! after more than threescore years and ten
  Of noble life blessed with pure love and sweet,
Gone from the places and the sight of men,
  Gathered like ripened corn or sheaf of wheat.

No loss of vigor, all undimmed the thought,
  Matchless the lustre of his latest verse,
With gems that are imperishable fraught;
  Since Shakespeare's whose so many-hued and terse?

Translated now into the higher sphere,
  Weep not for him, O ye, who loved him best,
United there to her he held most dear,
  Soul of his soul, "and with God be the rest ! " *

* From " Prospice "; —

        " Then a light, then thy breast
    O thou soul of my soul, I shall clasp thee again,
        And with God be the rest ! "

THOMAS WILLIAM PARSONS

LINES

WRITTEN AFTER READING "SURSUM CORDA," THE LAST POEM OF THOMAS WILLIAM PARSONS.

Whence came the peace? In truth thou knowest *now!*
  A peace immense that flooded all thy soul
  When " Sursum Corda " through the church did roll,
E'en as thou knelt and prayed with lifted brow,
Asperges me, and make as white as snow
Drifted in orchards when the winds do blow.
  Asperges me, a voice began to sing.
  And God to thy sad soul his peace did bring.
Soon thy worn spirit, lifted from its woe,
Made purer far than whitest " Wayland snow,"
  Cleaving the blue with strong, unfettered wings
  Soared like a lark, and still upsoaring sings.
Did Dante greet thee in the realm divine,
He whose high genius was the joy of thine?

Oct. 11, 1892.

59